The Book Bandit
Mystery of the Missing Books

By Ivan Solomon & Micah Groberman

 FriesenPress

Suite 300 - 990 Fort St
Victoria, BC, V8V 3K2
Canada

www.friesenpress.com

ISBN
978-1-5255-3224-5 (Hardcover)
978-1-5255-3225-2 (Paperback)
978-1-5255-3226-9 (eBook)

1. JUVENILE FICTION, ACTION & ADVENTURE

Distributed to the trade by The Ingram Book Company

The Book Bandit
Mystery of the Missing Books

By Ivan Solomon & Micah Groberman

THIS BOOK BELONGS TO:
Cupertino Library

Design & Artwork: Ivan   Photography: Micah   Story & Rhyme: Ivan & Micah

"Evan! Mila! It's time for bed.
Choose a good book" their mother said.

Evan told Mila, "it's my choice tonight."
He looked all around, but
there were no books in sight!

Mm

Mila sat down, in disbelief.
"Evan" she whispered, "I think there's a thief."

She peered out the window and covered a yawn,
Then noticed some books laying on the front lawn.

"Come on Evan, let's see where they lead,
Otherwise we'll have nothing to read."

They climbed out the window and followed the trail,
Bringing their wagon to collect every tale.

Up through the forest, with books all around,
They saw a raccoon reading one it had found.

"Mila!" yelled Evan,
"We've found the book thief!
He's a mask wearing critter with very sharp teeth."

"I'm a reading raccoon, not a thief or a crook,
I saw more up that mountain, let's go take a look."

So Mila and Evan and the raccoon,
Followed the trail by the light of the moon.

Up the mountain they climbed, getting icy and cold,
Finding more books than their cold hands could hold!

"Your wagon looks full" called an owl from above,
May I borrow a book 'cause it's reading I love."

"Evan and I would be happy to share,
Come back to our house, we can read them all there."

So Mila and Evan, the owl and raccoon
Followed the trail while all humming a tune.

B ack down the mountain with no thief in sight,
They came to a lake where a boat was tied tight.

Into the boat and across on the water,
Passing three mice and a book-reading otter.

Mila called out "Did you steal those books?"
"No" said the critters, "but we'll help find the crooks."

So the otter, the mice, the owl and raccoon,
All came along, hoping to find the thief soon.

Nursery Rhymes

Jack n the Beanstalk

Cinderella

Dictionary

PRINCESS and the PEA

THE HUNGRY HIPPO

Snake n Bake

Where the Monsters Go
Goodnight Moon

HORACE'S HOLIDAY

Chritmas Carol

TRUCKS & CARS

RUMPLESTILTSKIN

THE OWL and the PUSSYCAT
Charlot's Web

JUMBLE STORY
VOLUME 1

CAT IN THE HAT
KIDS STORIES

HUMPTY DUMPTY
Incy Wincy Spider

Three Blind Mice   VOLUME 2

RED ROCKET

Back on dry land with their wagon in tow,
Collecting more books from the trail as they go.

"Evan!" cried Mila, "Is that the thief there?"
"Who, me? Come on, I'm just a book-loving bear."

He had a book in his lap and sharp fangs in his smile,
But he said that he'd join them and search for a while.

So the raccoon and mice, otter, owl and bear,
All joined together to help out the pair.

Hissssssssssssss!

How to
Play
Snakes
&
Ladders

"What's that?" Evan shouted, hearing it first.
"The thief is a snake, oh what could be worse?"

"No mi amigosss, you've made a missssstake.
All I am hisss a book-reading sssssnake."

"Our books were all stolen" Evan said with a sigh.
"Can I help?" asked the snake, "I'm willing to try."

So the raccoon, owl and otter, three mice, snake and bear,
All worked together collecting books they could share.

Mila was tired and thought a rest would be best.
They all agreed and took a break from the quest.

The thief-searching friends huddled under a tree.
Perhaps finding the crook was not meant to be.

Then down from above came a **thump** and a **bump,**
Then **bump, thump, thump, bump,**
thump, bump, thump.

Book after book came down to the ground,
So they climbed up the tree without making a sound.

Hanging on to a branch,
and with wide open eyes,

They found the book thief,
Oh what a surprise!

"**A** worm?" Evan shouted, taking the lead,
"Don't be mad" said the worm, "I just love to read!"

"I'm a bookworm you see, but I truly do care,
I just didn't think you'd be willing to share."

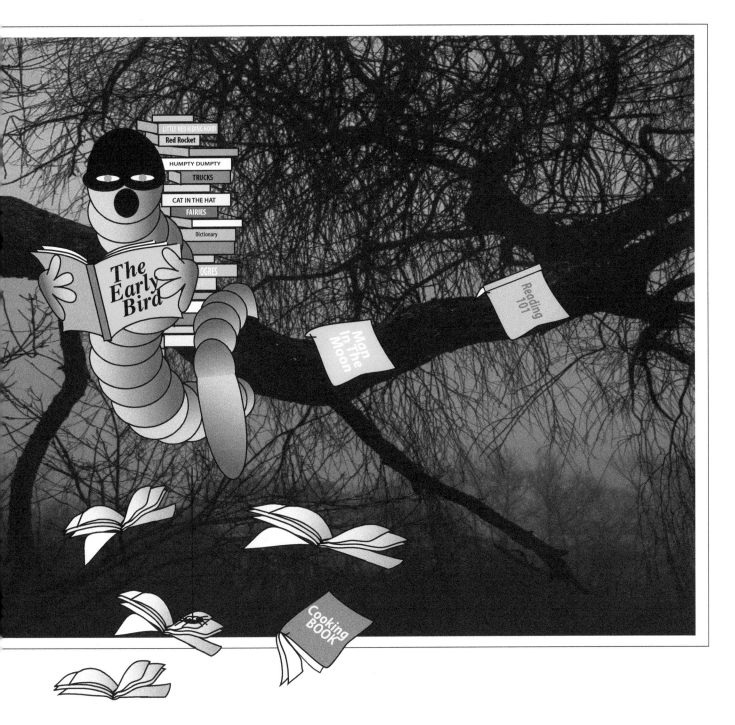

"You should ask," Mila said, "we'd lend you a book,
You really don't want to be known as a crook."

The bookworm said sorry and came down from the tree,
To help them pack up all the books they could see.

They made it back home, all by themselves,
And stocked all the books back onto their shelves.

The mystery was solved, it was now time for bed,
So they all chose a book that they hadn't yet read.

Zzz

The bookworm, the snake, the raccoon and the bear,
The owl, the otter and mice were all there.

Book reading friends that all learned to share,
As sharing's a great way to show that you care.

Stories at bedtime are certain to please,
Reading adventures that all end in Zzzzzzz's.

THE END

Animal Quiz

Bears sleep all winter long. What is this called?

Owls sleep all day and hunt at night. Owls are...?

Snakes eat meat. Snakes are....?

There are 18 spiders hiding in your book.
Did you find them all?

Painted Rocket Designs was created as a collaboration between two creative minds.
Internationally-renowned designer / artist / story teller / father / grandfather, **Ivan Solomon**
and photographer / creative writer / father / music & snack enthusiast, **Micah Groberman.**

To view their latest works of art, including
Book Bandit posters, art, games and much more...

paintedrocket.com

Acknowlegements:

IVAN - *Designer, illustrator, writer*

I dedicate this book to my grandchildren
Winston, King , Mila and soon to be 'King's
little sister,' who are my inspiration and who
have re-introduced me to the boundless
energy, creativity and endless imagination
of a childs mind. Thanks to my children
Amanda & Zachary for presenting me
with my wonderful grandchildren and to
Jeannie my soul partner who talked me
into having children in the first place.

MICAH - *Photographer, writer*

I would like to thank my loving, proof-
reading wife Maiky and my wonderful
kids Evan and Jonas for their inspiration,
advice and countless readings at home.
I love you very much. I would also like to
dedicate this book to my brother Jory, a
very important and positive influence on
my life, who encouraged me to write and
to my mom and dad, friends and family
for their advice, friendship and support.